Barbie™
Star for a Day
A Picture Scrapbook

VILLAGE CINEMA
RAPUNZEL
RATED G
5:00 PM, APRIL 12TH
ADMIT 1

By Mona Miller

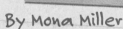

Cover photography: Willy Lew, Laura Lynch, Greg Roccia,
Terri Weber, Judy Tsuno, and Lisa Collins
Interior photography: Paul Jordan, Susan Kurtz, Glen Bradley,
Vince Okada, Judy Tsuno, Lisa Collins, and the Mattel Photo Studio

🌹 A GOLDEN BOOK • NEW YORK
Golden Books Publishing Company, Inc.,
New York, New York 10106

Library of Congress Catalog Card Number: 00-106815   ISBN: 0-307-10625-X
First Edition 2001
10 9 8 7 6 5 4 3 2 1

My Scrapbook

I love to feel like a star, whether I'm dancing in a ballet or working at a fashion show. It takes a lot of practice and hard work, but it's worth it! This picture scrapbook captures some of my special moments in the spotlight.

Barbie

ADMIT ONE

SWAN LAKE

SEC: ORCHESTRA

ROW: C **SEAT: 14**

DATE: JANUARY 8TH

TIME: 8:00 PM

Here's a ticket from my first ballet performance.

I had a wonderful time modeling in this fashion show.

Barbie Fashion Show OFFICIAL PROGRAM

January 8th—My Dream Ballet

It was a dream come true when I got to dance in Swan Lake. I had imagined myself in that ballet ever since I took my first dance class. I felt lighter than air as I leaped and pirouetted across the stage to the music.

My sisters gave me a bouquet of yellow roses after the show.

I practiced hard every day.

I love to get fan mail.

Dear Barbie,
   You were wonderful in the show tonight! I can't believe how graceful you are. Someday I hope I can be a ballerina just like you!
                    Your favorite fan,
                              Catie

It's great to be appreciated for my hard work.

Barbie's Feet Take Flight in *Swan Lake*!

Barbie set the stage on fire with a brilliant performance of *Swan Lake* this evening.
   Her dancing and acting were outstanding and had the audience begging for more!

When I got the lead role in the play Sleeping Beauty, I had to learn all my lines in just two weeks—and go to rehearsals every night! But it was worth it. The play was a huge success.

I loved the gold crown and the pretty costume that I wore.

PROGRAM

Fairy Tale Theatre
Sleeping Beauty
Starring
Barbie

Theatre Review January / February

Barbie Brings Down the House in *Sleeping Beauty!*

BALCONY A 20

SLEEPING BEAUTY

BAL

A 20

FAIRY TALE THEATRE
FEBRUARY 14
7:00 PM

14 FEB

14 FEB

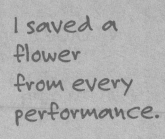

These are my friends' ticket stubs. I love performing when they're in the audience.

I saved a flower from every performance.

April 12th—My First Movie

It's amazing how one thing leads to another! A movie director saw Sleeping Beauty and said that she had the perfect role for me—Rapunzel! The movie was filmed at a real castle with a lovely garden, and I got to wear lots of pretty princess dresses.

Making this movie was the most fun I've ever had!

VILLAGE CINEMA
RAPUNZEL
RATED G
5:00 PM, APRIL 12TH
ADMIT 1

ADMIT 1

Here are some tickets from my first movie!

It takes a long time to put on makeup before each take.

It's great to get a praising review.

Thumbs Up for Barbie in The Story of Rapunzel!

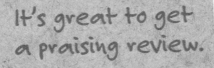

June 20th—On the Runway

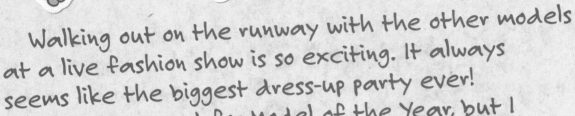

   Walking out on the runway with the other models at a live fashion show is so exciting. It always seems like the biggest dress-up party ever!

   I won an award for Model of the Year, but I accepted the trophy on behalf of all the other models who had worked just as hard as I had.

I had a great time working with my friends on this show.

August 26th—Dressing Up

Being a model is not as easy as it looks. I spend hours at photo shoots in studios and faraway places. It also takes time to pick out clothes with the designers and to make sure that they fit me just right.

Modeling clothes is fun because I can pretend to be a different person in each outfit.

These are my favorite hair clips!

Here are some of the shots we took at my last photo shoot.

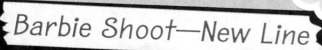
Barbie Shoot—New Line

October 6th—Designing Clothes

I like dressing up so much that I started designing some clothes of my own. This outfit is one of my favorites. A famous designer liked it so much that he put it in one of his fashion shows.

I was thrilled when the audience clapped and cheered for my design.

It's fun choosing different fabrics for my designs.

I had a great time designing this fashion line.

October 31st—Costume Party

Sometimes I like to design clothes and costumes just for fun. I made this sparkling princess costume for a Halloween ball. And Ken looked so dashing as my prince.

I kept a souvenir from the party.

Here are some pictures from the party. This was such a great night.

Please Join Us!

For: Halloween Party

Date: October 31st

Time: 8 pm

Place: The Haunted House

November 8th—Special Report

The local TV station asked me to do a special report on fashion. I got to interview many famous models and designers.

I was a little nervous at the thought of being on television. But I did lots of research, and I practiced speaking in front of the camera. My show turned out great!

BUZZTV3

Dear Barbie,
  We would love for you to join our news crew to do a special report covering fashion trends and personalities from around the world. It would be an exciting opportunity for you to travel and meet

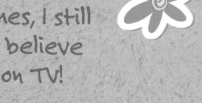

At times, I still can't believe I was on TV!

December 15th—On the News

The TV station liked my fashion report and asked me to continue reporting. I've interviewed so many interesting people—even a real-life princess!

The best part of being a reporter is letting people know about really important things, like the opening of the new Children's Medical Center.

THIS WEEK'S TV

Special R

Barbie brings us a report from the Children's Medical Center where she interviews Princess Julia in her first trip to the United States.

port from Barbie!

The spotlight can be a lot of fun, but the everyday things can make me feel like a star, too. When Ken and I go dancing, it's like the world is a stage and we're the only two people on it.

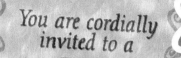

You are cordially
invited to a

New Year's Eve GALA BALL

December 31st at 9pm
Rose Ballroom
Hors d'Oeuvres, Dinner
Please RSVP

I saved our invitation from this dance as a memento of a special evening.

My corsage was beautiful!

What's your favorite star moment?

Glue or tape a favorite photo of yourself here. Or you can draw a picture if you like.